DATE DUE

APR 1 7 2006	
NOV 1 5 2018	

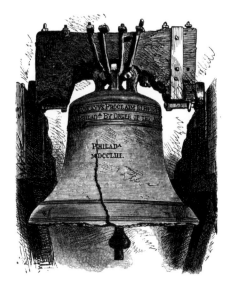

Give *Me*
Liberty

by Diana Star Helmer

Perfection Learning®

Cover Illustration: Dan Hatala
Inside Illustration: Michael Aspengren pp. 27, 29, 33, 45
              Dan Hatala pp. 4, 23, 30, 39, 47;

Art Credits: Art Today: Title Page, pp. 3, 5, 7, 9, 10, 11, 12, 13, 14, 15, 16, 17, 18, 19, 20, 24, 25, 31, 35, 36, 37, 42, 43, 46, 48, 49, 51, 52, 54, 55, 56; Dover: pp. 6, 41; Library of Congress: pp. 7, 34, 53; North Wind Picture Archives: p. 8

Dedication

To Pat and Fred McKissack, remembering one fine afternoon just hanging around together

About the Author

Diana Star Helmer grew up in Iowa. She loved fireflies, tall autumn skies, bright snowy nights, and waiting for spring. But she wondered about the ocean, the mountains, and all kinds of art in the city.

She moved near Seattle, Washington, and five happy years later, she suddenly got homesick. So she went home to Iowa with her husband, Thomas S. Owens, who is also an author of children's books. A white cat came to their house one day and never left.

Ms. Helmer loves writing and thinking and drawing and dancing and, of course, Tom and Angel.

For information, contact
Perfection Learning® Corporation, 1000 North Second Avenue, P.O. Box 500, Logan, Iowa 51546-0500.
Phone: 1-800-831-4190 • Fax: 1-712-644-2392

Paperback ISBN 0-7891-5078-6
Cover Craft® ISBN 0-7807-9042-1

8 9 10 11 12 PP 08 07 06 05 04

Contents

Chapter 1

Hunting

Days like this made me feel as if we were friends.

"Let's stop to eat," Will said.

I wished he'd said it sooner. We had been hunting all morning.

I handed him the bag of food. Will took what he wanted. Then he handed it back.

"Moses, I don't even like hunting. Not since British soldiers moved into Virginia," Will said.

Will chewed on a chunk of pork jerky. "They could be anywhere."

"They wear red coats," I reminded him. "We'd see them before they saw us."

Will's face did not relax. It almost never did.

"The fighting is closer all the time," he said. "And I'm old enough to be a soldier."

"But you don't see well enough to shoot," I said.

"I know," Will said. "But Father doesn't know that. Thanks to you."

I always went hunting with Will. We told Master Stone that Will shot whatever we brought home. But Will would be lucky to shoot a house even if he stood in it. The eyeglasses Will wore no longer helped much.

And no ships had carried new glass for months.

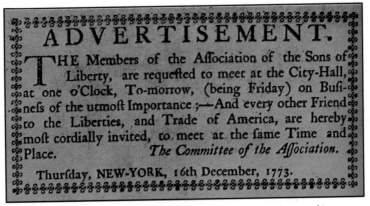

"You think your father's against the British?" I asked.

Will nodded. "Father remembers England. He says life is good there. But only if you're rich.

"Jobs for the poor pay just enough to buy food. The poor can't better themselves.

"That's why Father came here. Anyone can make money and live well."

That's not true, I thought.

"The colonists—the Sons of Liberty—are fighting because they don't want the king taking our money. And telling us what to do," Will continued. "Father read it in the newspaper. I memorized some of it."

> ## ADVERTISEMENT.
>
> THE Members of the Affociation of the Sons of Liberty, are requefted to meet at the City-Hall, at one o'Clock, To-morrow, (being Friday) on Bufi-nefs of the utmoft Importance ;—And every other Friend to the Liberties, and Trade of America, are hereby moft cordially invited, to meet at the fame Time and Place. *The Committee of the Affociation.*
>
> Thurfday, NEW-YORK, 16th December, 1773.

Note that the letter *s* often looks like the letter *f.*

Remembering was easier for Will than reading with bad eyes.

"Father read, 'We hold these truths to be self-evident, that all men are created equal.' "

I knew Will's father did not believe that.

"And it's true!" Will said. "Look at what Father has gained in America. And he just makes barrels."

I knew the story. Will's father didn't have enough money to ride the boat here from England. But he knew that people in the colonies got rich selling tobacco.

So Will's father rode the boat. Once here, he asked a tobacco farmer to pay for his passage. In return, Will's father had to work for that farmer for seven years.

Will's father, Master Stone, made barrels for Master Fox. Barrels were used to ship tobacco from the colonies to England.

After seven years, Master Stone had paid his debt. But he kept making barrels for Master Fox. Only now, he was paid. And Master Stone saved that money to buy his own land.

"Father could never have owned land in England," Will said. "Here, he could. And the little farm fed us. Father could keep saving. He wanted his own tobacco farm. So, when he had saved enough—"

"He bought me," I said.

"That's right, Moses," Will said. "He bought you."

Chapter 2

Caught!

I have not heard my name since I was tall as the Master's hip. At least I have not heard my real name.

I must be about 15 years old now. That's the same age as Will.

But I know I could still speak my first language. Sometimes, I think I hear one of those words. Of course, it's only English. Then I feel homesick.

Hot sun makes me homesick too. But I'm homesick for what? I've been so long from home. I can't even remember my mother's face.

"By now, Father hoped to save enough to plant tobacco. Then you would work the farm," Will said. "Not just chores.

"But Father hasn't saved enough. England keeps taxing us more," Will continued. "They say tax money pays the King's soldiers. And they keep our colonies safe."

"But England takes too much. The poor stay poor. The colonies will soon be like England. Unless we fight."

I wished the colonies were like England. In England, there were no slaves.

I did not pretend Will and I were friends anymore that day. We were master and slave, eating and hunting.

I carried home the four geese I shot. Will's father met us at the gate.

"Good shooting today," he said.

"Yes, sir," Will nodded.

"Edward Greene was hunting today." Master looked at Will, hard. "Said he saw Moses here take down some geese."

Will only blinked. Master Stone's face tightened.

"So, it's true. Boy, what are you thinking? Teaching a slave to shoot! Haven't you seen the newspapers?"

He stopped because he didn't want me to know. But I knew. Sometimes, slaves shot and killed their masters. Then they ran away, hoping for freedom.

Master Stone grabbed the gun. "I have no use for a slave who can shoot. But the Sons of Liberty will. They're asking every family to send at least one soldier."

I stopped breathing. Master was sending me away forever.

Maybe soldiers made money. Maybe they made enough to buy freedom!

"But, Father," Will said. "Does the army take black soldiers?"

Master Stone snorted. "The army will take anyone who stays. At least until the war is over. The army is small because no one is paid. Nobody stays long. But Moses—"

He turned on me. "You'll have no place to go. You can't come back. You can't run anywhere. Not without freedom papers. And you won't get those till the war is over."

But then I'd be free. If I could just live through a war, I would be free.

Chapter

3

A Tangled Web

Master Stone didn't want me in his house another day. He knew I could shoot, and that bothered him.

But Mistress begged that I stay two weeks. At least until I finished the cloth I was weaving.

I was one of the best weavers in the county. The best, really, Mistress said. But she said I shouldn't brag.

Like most farmers, Master Stone always planted flax. We made cloth from it.

Planting and picking was done by the men of the house. That included Master, his two brothers, Will, and me.

Mistress and I cleaned and combed the stringy plant. The spinning wheel twisted and stretched it into thread. Then we wove the thread into cloth.

When I was little, I danced whenever Mistress worked the loom. I thought I remembered dancing in my first home. It was somewhere far away.

But here, I was the Stones' only slave. As I grew, there was no one to dance with.

But by then, I could weave. Mistress taught me when my fingers were tiny and quick.

I easily threaded the wooden loom for strong twill cloth or fancy linen. And I wanted to learn.

When I pressed one pedal on the loom, it raised a set of threads. I threw a shuttle of thread under them. Then I quickly pressed my other foot.

The first threads lowered. New threads raised. The shuttle flew to my other hand. Hand and foot. Back and forth. I felt like I was dancing.

Soon, I did all the weaving. Mistress spun the thread. We made cloth as fine as any from England. We even sold our extra.

But Master still worked for the day he could plant more tobacco and less flax.

"Tobacco is the way to riches," he had said. Even though tobacco meant buying more slaves. And they would have to be fed and clothed.

As I wove that last cloth, I wished I could weave forever. Yet I wished I could leave tomorrow. Then I could start my new life right away.

Mistress sewed nearby. "You used to dance when I wove."

She remembered? I thought.

"You wouldn't dance for anyone but me," she said.

I had wanted freedom since the day I came here. How could I think I might miss the people who had made me a slave?

Mistress pushed her work aside. "Moses, come here."

She held the sewing to me. "I wanted to surprise you. But you keep growing. And it won't fit unless I tell you now."

It was a soldier's uniform.

I couldn't speak. Hired hands get money or clothes when they leave. But no one gave a suit to a slave, especially a new suit.

In two weeks, I'd have a new master. In fact, I would have an army of masters. But Mistress's gift almost made me feel free that day.

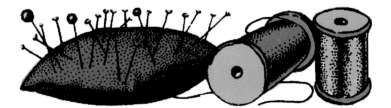

Chapter

Fighting
for Freedom

Later, I plucked feathers from the dead
geese. But my head was like a
honeycomb running over with sweetness.
"When are you leaving?"
Angel's bare feet had made no sound.

Angel was about my age. She wasn't sure of her age, though. Most slaves weren't.

"How'd you know?" I asked.

"I heard your master tell my Master Fox."

"Did you hear I'll be free after the war?"

"That's why I came." Angel sat. She started ripping out feathers. "We talked before about . . . maybe marrying. If the masters let us."

"Seems like they would. The law says slaves can't see each other. But they let us." I wiped my hands on my pants before reaching into my pocket. "I even made this for you."

Angel wiped her hands before she took the little cloth. "That's a fine piece of weaving, Moses."

I looked down. "When we get married, I'll make cloth like that for a dress."

"But you're going to be free," Angel said. "If you live through this war."

"I'll come back and buy your freedom," I said.

"No." Angel stood. "Don't come back. I don't trust your master."

"But he's good to us!" I said.

21

"Only to get my master's friendship! If you and I married, our children would belong to my master. They'd be his slaves. They would make money for him," Angel said.

"And money is why you're going to the army. It's not because you can shoot. It's so young Will won't have to go."

I nodded. "Master Stone told me. Every family sends one soldier."

"Family?" Angel's eyes widened. "I know you always talk for Will. But since when are you his brother?"

"The army doesn't want you. It wants Master Stone. Or Will. But Master Stone doesn't want Will getting killed. He wants a son to leave his money to."

"Why should I care?" I asked. "I'll still be free."

"Not if you come back," Angel said. "Moses, men who believe in freedom fight for it.

"Master Stone is sending you to do the job for him. A job!" She kicked some feathers. "Like plucking geese."

"You don't get freedom for plucking," Angel said. "And he might not give you freedom for fighting."

"The army will give me freedom papers!" I said.

"What if two white men here tell a judge you belong to Master Stone? Your papers won't matter," she said. "It won't matter what you say. Not even what Mistress Stone says. Just two white men. And a freed black is a slave again. Just like that."

Angel turned away for a moment. Then she put the piece of cloth on my knee.

"Don't come back," she whispered.

Her feet were quiet as she left.

Slave Chain.

Chapter 5

Believe

Angel had stripped my hopes almost as bare as I had stripped those geese.

I would never be truly free. I'd be fighting for freedom my whole life. Even after the war, I'd be fighting

Anyplace I went, two white men could make me a slave again. All they had to say was that I belonged to someone.

My only hope was to come back here. These good white men—the Stones— would defend me.

Or would they? Or was Angel right?

I heard Master calling. He'd just come home. He had two children—a boy and a girl. They were both black.

I felt cold.

"Since you're staying two weeks, I thought you could teach my new help their jobs," Master said. He spied Mistress at the door.

"Look!" Master crowed. "Got a good price. Because they're small. Like when I bought Moses. They'll grow. Just like he did.

"And they aren't brother and sister. They might have children later. Save us from buying more."

The little ones had held hands till Master said that. Now the boy pulled away. Tears rolled down the girl's cheeks.

Mistress's face tightened. She took the children's hands. She knew the law made men masters.

Women were not governors. Women could not vote. Like me, Mistress did as she was told.

She led the children inside. Master followed, talking happily.

Will came from the house. He had ink on his fingers.

"I heard voices," he said. "I was adding the family budget."

"You'll have to subtract some," I said quietly. "Your father just bought two slaves."

"Well." Will blinked. "That's good, I guess. Since we won't have you to work."

I finally burst. "I thought your Sons of Liberty believed 'all men are created equal.' How can you have slaves?"

49	42	90	81
612	50	109	25
25	08	6	12
264	37	52	99
80	12	2,372	20
119	02	104	62
53	10	87	09
2	91	224	25
18	44	314	15
1,710	09	912	11
20	03	283	55
362	50	65	20
75	22	25	08
462	87	318	06
110	20	16	57
204	43	800	04
387	09	922	75
2,186	11	6,142	27
2	02	9	05
10	80	1,500	00
127	70	450	16
86	09	742	34
32	27	400	04
486	11	27	11

"Aren't we people? Same as you?"

"Well . . . of course. . . . You're people," Will stammered. "But . . . you're a . . . a different kind of people. The good Lord put you here to serve. You can't help it your people aren't as smart."

"Not smart?" I glared at Will. "Who can weave here? You or me?"

Will hated talking. He hated arguing even more. His face was red. So was his voice.

"Dogs can do some jobs too. But dogs still aren't people," Will looked at his shoes. "Except . . . I'm glad you're not like other people. I can't talk to people. I can talk to you."

I didn't care. "All men are created equal," I said. I pointed to his paper. "I'll prove it. That's your name. Stone. It's written right there."

Will blinked. "Well. It's my paper. Anyone would know it's my name."

I took a breath, then pointed to each letter, saying its name.

"Well," Will said after a moment. "Well. Still . . . knowing letters isn't reading. Besides, you might just remember the sounds from hearing Mama teach me."

I stared for a long moment. Finally I picked up a feather. I pressed the quill into the dirt. Then I wrote four words.

Chapter

Seeing Is Believing

That night, I slept with the little ones. Their names were Peter and Bessie.

Years ago, I'd hated sleeping in the barn. I was so far from everyone.

But the cow's breathing was close and warm. And a cow is as good a listener as Mistress. And better than Will.

Will didn't talk much. But I never knew just how much he really heard.

Peter and Bessie couldn't sleep yet.

"When was you sold?" asked Bessie.

"My mama belongs to Master Lee. Ten miles off," Peter said. "Where's yours?"

I liked talking. I didn't mind that they were young.

I'd never talked much with other slaves, except Angel. She'd told me about other slaves. But that's different from being together.

I heard footsteps. Will's shadow stepped inside.

Peter and Bessie saw too. "What have we done?"

"Hush, now," I said.

"Moses?" Will's voice shook. He didn't like being near new folks. Even if they were children. "Moses, I can't figure how you wrote that. I remember you studied with me once. Years ago. But Mama gave up teaching you. You couldn't learn."

I grinned in the moonlight. "You don't remember. We studied together till Master saw us. I couldn't read words yet. But I could read faces.

"He was mad because I was there with you. And I was learning.

"So I scribbled a mess on your slate. Then I said, 'A, B, C!'"

"Your mother said, 'See? He isn't learning. He's just a little parrot.' But Master said he didn't want a parrot spoiling your lessons."

Will nodded. "Mama must have taught you to weave then. Seems you always wove during studies. Could you hear the lessons in there?"

"Some," I said. "But mostly, Mistress taught me early mornings. Or we'd read cooking books together when you and Master were out."

Will pushed up his eyeglasses. "Mama must be a fine teacher. To teach you! An African! I never heard of a slave who could read."

"I can say my ABCs," Bessie whispered.

"I thought you were asleep," I said. But in the darkness, she started saying letters.

"Hush!" Peter hissed. "You'll get us in trouble."

"No!" said Will. His voice was suddenly calm. "It's all right. I won't tell. I know it's against the law to teach slaves. But I think it's good you're so smart. Smart workers are better workers."

"Workers?" I said. "Workers get paid."

"Did we just prove that we're equal to workers? Or are we still slaves?"

"Moses." Will's voice was pained. "You're slaves. Because you don't know the word of God."

"I do!" Bessie piped. "I know Bible words. 'Thou shall not steal.' 'Thou shall not kill.' "

I looked hard at Will. " 'Blessed are they who hunger for right, for they shall be filled.' "

Chapter 7

Taking Sides

Will was silent a long, long time.

In the darkness, Bessie whispered to Peter. "Everybody says Will lets Moses do all his talking. Maybe that's why Will wants to know if we're smart. Maybe we'll do his talking after Moses leaves."

Will stood. "I suppose I've got to do some talking for myself," he said. He walked out.

Next morning, I heard hollering while I milked the cow. It was Master.

"I don't care what he can read or spell! That boy belongs to me. I paid good money for him. I'll decide what he does and where he goes."

Through the barn door, I could see Will. He stood by the house. His voice was as pale as his face. I couldn't hear what he said. Just Master's voice.

"Someone from this family has to go. Your uncles and I have too much work here. And what if the fighting comes any closer? We may have to defend the farm."

Will's next words were short.

"You're not going anywhere!" Master yelled. "You're my only son. Without you, this place will die when I die. Your mother couldn't keep up a farm alone. Without you or me, she'd have to sell. Moses is going, and that's final. What's more—"

Master turned and marched toward me in the barn. I almost ran.

"You're leaving today," Master barked. "I don't want you here another day. I don't want you putting ideas into Will's head. And I don't want him putting thoughts into yours."

He stomped back to the house. Will stood at the barn door.

"I'm sorry," he whispered. "I tried to tell him you should be free. Because you know the Bible. But . . . well. You'll still be free. After the war."

"If I live," I said. "And what about Peter? And Bessie?"

Will blinked.

"Should they be slaves? Knowing what they know?"

"Moses," Will's eyes begged. "He's my father."

I didn't move. "I guess he's your master too. But today, Will? Today, he's not my master anymore. I'm already free. Because I'm off to fight for freedom.

"And you know what I'm going to do? First chance? I'm going to run away from the rebel army. And I will join the British!"

Will turned pale. "The Tories? Why?"

"They don't have slaves. They are not like your Sons of Liberty. In England, I will always be free. No matter what any man says."

Chapter

Give Me Liberty

I was on my way.

Mistress, Bessie, and Peter cried when I left. They held one another.

My uniform was still pinned in a place or two. I would have to finish sewing it myself.

Master Stone shoved my paper at me. The letter said who I was. And where I was going. Whites who could read would know I wasn't running away.

Will didn't even come to say good-bye.

I knew I could write another pass. One that would give me freedom now. All I needed was a pen and ink.

But I'd be running all my life that way. From the two white men who could make me a slave. No. I'd join the Sons of Liberty today. And someday, when we were close to the British, I'd go join them instead. In England, I'd be free.

I heard footsteps behind mine.

It was Will. He was carrying bags. And his gun.

He stopped and pushed up his eyeglasses. "It takes two soldiers to fire a cannon," he said. "I think I see well enough to load. Someone else just has to aim."

We walked together awhile.

"You can go straight to the British. If that's what you want," Will said quietly. "I'll be joining the rebels. I figure we'll even out the sides that way."

We walked awhile more.

"Will?" I said. "There may not be slaves in England. But the British bring slaves here from Africa to sell. I can't count on someone treating me right, just because he's British. I just have to see how someone treats me. So . . . I guess I'll join the rebels with you. And I'll stay."

"Moses, really?" Will's eyes were begging again. "I had to do this. You can't fight for my freedom. I have to fight for it myself.

"But I'm so scared, Moses. All those people. Would you stay with me? I think the army will let you. If . . . if you'd let me say you're mine.

"The truth of it is, I'm at your mercy, Moses. I don't know if I can do this alone."

I looked ahead as we walked. "Will you pay me back?"

"How?"

"If we win this war, I need help. My freedom won't last without a white man's help," I said. "You'll probably go back to the farm. But I'd like to be somewhere else."

"I could never run a tobacco farm," Will said. "Even before I understood about you. Or about how Father was building the place.

"I always knew a big farm needed more slaves. And I don't want lots of people,

Moses. I just want someplace small.

"Maybe you and I could have a shop," Will continued. "We could sell your cloth. I could figure the money. And I would only be around people enough to keep you out of trouble."

He grinned so I would know he was joking.

I had to grin too. I liked the idea of weaving again. And I had a feeling that Will and I might be friends.

"You suppose we might make enough money to maybe buy someone's freedom?" I said.

Will didn't look at me. "Angel?" he asked.

I nodded. "Could we stop by the Fox place on our way? There's something I want to give her."

Will grinned. "I know. That special weaving you made."

I nodded. But there was something else I wanted Angel to have.

Hope.

Chapter 9

Liberty and Justice for All?

Africans lived in the American colonies almost from the start. Few, if any, came by choice.

African villagers sometimes kidnapped people from other villages. Then they would sell the captives to white men. Many of these white men were English.

In 1772, slavery was banned in England. But British ships still carried hundreds of slaves to the colonies.

Starting in 1619, blacks in the colonies were expected to work without pay for a set number of years. Then these indentured servants were set free.

Poor white people were often indentured servants, too, like Master Stone. They worked to pay a debt such as passage to the colonies. Once the debt was paid, they were free.

By 1700, however, lifelong slavery of blacks was a colonial way of life. And it was the law.

Blacks still became free sometimes. Especially during the Revolutionary War (1775–1783). Some were set free to fight for the Sons of Liberty. Others were sent as substitute soldiers for white colonists.

Still others fought for the British. The slaves were promised freedom after the war. But nothing really changed.

After the war, just like before, a free black could be recaptured. Then he was forced to work as a slave again.

Many slaves worked on farms. Most farms were small. They had few slaves or none.

But big farms, or plantations, often had many slaves. They had to build and dig, plant and harvest, cook, clean, weave, and sew.

Slaves were not paid. Money made from slaves' work went right to the masters' pockets. These masters could then afford fine clothes, houses, and good schooling for their sons.

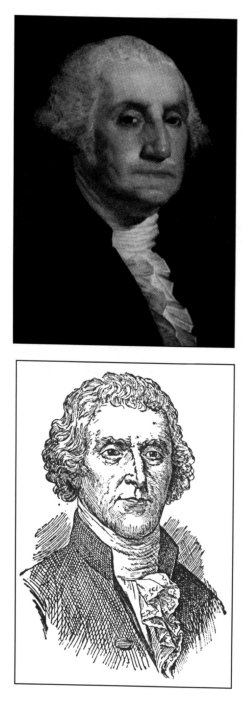

America's first president, General George Washington, was from such a family. So was Thomas Jefferson. Jefferson wrote the Declaration of Independence. It said "all men are created equal."

Both Washington and Jefferson owned slaves. How could people who fought for freedom take it away from others?

John Hancock signing the Declaration of Independence

Such owners tried to fool themselves. Most colonists were church-going Christians. They thought that it was all right to enslave non-Christians.
The owners felt that anyone who didn't know about their God wasn't really a person yet.

So owners had to keep slaves from learning about their God. If slaves became Christian, they would have to go free.

Laws were passed. These said blacks could not learn to read. They couldn't learn to write either. Freedom papers were written like everything else. By hand!

But from the beginning, many people knew slavery was wrong. And when the Sons of Liberty won the war, the colonies became a democracy.

Now colonists could change laws. That is if enough colonists agreed. Antislavery groups tried to convince owners to change the laws and stop slavery.

The talking went on until 1861 when the talk turned into war. American against American. When the Civil War ended in 1865, so did slavery.

But a country is truly free only when people let one another be free. Even after slavery ended, the fight for freedom and equality went on.